MYLES

and the

MONSTER OUTSIDE

WEIRD STORIES GONE WRONG

MYLES

and the

MONSTER OUTSIDE

PHILIPPA DOWDING

Illustrations by Shawna Daigle

DUNDURN
TORONTO

Project Editor: Carrie Gleason   Editor: Allister Thompson
Illustrator: Shawna Daigle   Cover Design: Courtney Horner
Cover art by Shawna Daigle
Printer: Webcom

Library and Archives Canada Cataloguing in Publication
Dowding, Philippa, 1963-, author
     Myles and the monster outside / Philippa Dowding(Weird stories gone wrong)
Issued in print and electronic formats.
ISBN 978-1-4597-2943-8 (pbk.).--ISBN 978-1-4597-2944-5 (pdf).--
ISBN 978-1-4597-2945-2 (epub)

     I. Title. II. Series: Dowding, Philippa, 1963- Weird stories
gone wrong

PS8607.O9874M95 2015   jC813'.6   C2015-900587-6
                                                                        C2015-900588-4

1   2   3   4   5   19   18   17   16   15

We acknowledge the support of the **Canada Council for the Arts** and the **Ontario Arts Council** for our publishing program. We also acknowledge the financial support of the **Government of Canada** through the **Canada Book Fund** and **Livres Canada Books**, and the **Government of Ontario** through the **Ontario Book Publishing Tax Credit** and the **Ontario Media Development Corporation**.

Care has been taken to trace the ownership of copyright material used in this book. The author and the publisher welcome any information enabling them to rectify any references or credits in subsequent editions.

J. Kirk Howard, President
The publisher is not responsible for websites or their content unless they are owned by the publisher. Printed and bound in Canada.

VISIT US AT
Dundurn.com | @dundurnpress | Facebook.com/dundurnpress | Pinterest.com/dundurnpress

Dundurn
3 Church Street, Suite 500
Toronto, Ontario, Canada
M5E 1M2

For those in the back seat,
who see things no one else can

THIS PART IS (MOSTLY) TRUE …

You should know, before you even start this book, that it's a little scary. And parts of it are even a bit strange. I wish I could make the story less scary and strange, but this is the way I heard it, so I really have no choice.

It starts like this:

A long time ago, a beautiful dog got lost in the rain.

The dog's owner loved him very much and couldn't bear to lose him. So even though it was a stormy spring night, the old man put on his rich leather shoes and his expensive coat and went to search for his beloved dog.

The old man looked all through the fields and dark woods around his home. The rain fell, but still he walked further and further through marshes, swamps, and soaking meadows in the dark. But it was no use. His dog seemed lost for good.

So the old man turned his back to the fields and swamps and searched out by the highway. He walked alone along the dark, rainy road. He never found his dog (this is definitely the sad part). You should know that the dog turned up at home the next day, safe and sound. In fact, unlike his owner, he lived a long, happy life.

Here's the strange part. No one saw the old man again. He just wandered off and disappeared. That seems to be the truth of it, but no one likes a story to end that way. People usually want some kind of a proper ending they can believe in. Some people like a happy ending. Certain kinds of people will choose a spooky ending, every time.

So, in this story, the first kind of person will say that the old man was rich enough to wander away to somewhere warm and pleasant. Florida, perhaps.

But the second type of person will tell you this: the old man died of a broken heart. They may go on to say that many, many years later on rainy spring nights, the old man's spirit still walks the highway. And if you want to hear the truth (as scary as it may be), the ghostly old man waves down strangers in lonely cars to ask if they have seen his dog.

No one ever has.

Except once.

I'll be getting to that part soon.

You don't have to believe this story. But just because things are odd or a little strange or unbelievable doesn't always make them untrue. Truth is an odd thing; one person's truth can be another person's lie. That's the most important thing to remember about this story: sometimes things that seem like lies are actually true. And sometimes you never can tell.

That's the spookiest thing of all.

CHAPTER 1

MONSTER ISLAND

Myles leaned against the ship's railing. There was nothing to see but grey water, grey sky, and grey, misty islands. Or rocks that passed as islands.

All the empty grey worried Myles. Where was land? A huge, icy wave splashed up into his face. Myles spluttered.

It was windy and cold, too.

No one else was on the ferry because most normal people — tourists — only travelled on it in the *summer*. No one in their right mind would do it *now*, in the middle of April. It was freezing cold, raining, and there was nothing to see.

Plus the water was very choppy. On top of being worried, Myles was also starting to feel a little seasick.

The man who sold French fries (seasick!) at the snack bar inside the ship told Myles that in the summer, the ferry was a nice ride. The islands were covered with green bushes and wild blueberries. One island was called "Flower Pot Island" because of the towering limestone rocks with wildflowers on top. But right now, in April, the islands all looked the same: grey, dead, and covered in foggy mist.

The churning water and the misty islands also looked a little … spooky. Anything could be out there, waiting, in the misty grey.

Which was upsetting. But not nearly as upsetting as his next thought.

"I wish I was back at my old home with my friends. I'm going to hate Nobleville, and I haven't even been there yet," Myles whispered to the grey, misty air.

There, he'd said it. Saying it didn't help untie the knot in his stomach, though.

He turned and looked through the cabin window. He could see his older sister Bea and his little brother Norman leaning on either side of their mother inside the ferry.

They looked warm. And dry.

But it was better to be outside in the cold, grey mist than inside with his family. Four days stuck inside a smelly, garbage-filled car together was enough to drive anyone crazy.

And one family member wasn't even with them. Myles's dad. He was already in their new town, in their new house, working at his new job so the family could enjoy a "better life." Myles wasn't sure what that meant, exactly, but he hoped it included a room of his own and a dog.

Although it probably didn't.

It DID mean a new school for Myles, though.

Suddenly his stomach felt even worse.

Thanks a lot, Dad, for making us move across the country.

Another huge wave hit the side of the ship, and Myles got soaked. He turned around and saw Norman staring at him through the window. Myles made a face at his little brother.

He was SO sick of Norman.

"I want to go home," Myles whispered once more into the mist.

He stared over the water and worried, because there was plenty to worry about. He sank deeper into his gloom.

Suddenly, an island loomed out of the fog. It was closer than the others, and Myles could see black, dripping trees and swirling mist. The island rose from the dark water like a strange ship or a house. But there was something different about this island. He could see it quite clearly, it was so close to him. He could almost reach out and touch the nearest trees.

Myles looked closer.

Something moved on the shore!

Myles blinked and looked again. The island was quickly disappearing into the fog, but there was definitely *something standing on the rocks.*

And it was *looking* at him.

Myles gasped.

The thing looked like a man. It couldn't be a *man*, though, because it was huge. No man could be that big. Plus, it was … misty. There was no other word for it. It swirled in the grey like fog as it formed into the shape of a man. The misty man-shape moved across the rocks.

The word *monster* whispered in Myles's head. He backed up across the ferry deck.

He blinked again.

No denying it this time.

Something huge and grey skulked across the shore. It moved fast toward the water, like a cloud. The grey, misty form turned and looked at him.

Myles held his breath.

It *was* an enormous man made of fog and mist, with huge, wispy legs, a swirling grey chest, and long, floating arms. Misty fingers reached toward the water. In the centre of the face swirled two bright RED EYES.

Like fire.

Myles tried not to scream. He bit his tongue and his heart hammered painfully in his chest.

The monster stood at the water's edge and looked at him. It raised its grey head and sniffed the air. Then it slipped below the waves.

A trail of bubbles started toward the ferry.

CHAPTER 2

VICTOR-THE-VOLVO

What IS that thing?

Myles bolted into the seating area, the heavy glass door slamming behind him. The sudden warmth and brightness inside the ship made him stop. The old wooden benches had just been painted, and the place smelled like oil paint, bubble gum, and greasy French fries.

It made Myles's stomach lurch even more.

He darted over to his mother, Bea, and Norman, who rested his head on his mother's shoulder. Bea was reading and ignored the world beyond her book, as always. Myles's mother was snoring gently. He didn't have the heart to wake her up. He knew she had hardly slept since they left home. Hotel rooms weren't very comfortable, especially if there was just one bed, a pull-out couch, and four people.

Myles looked around. What had he just seen? Who should he tell? The other adults on the ferry, the few that there were, all read their newspapers or had their eyes closed like his mother.

What would he say, anyway? *There's ... uh ... a huge, grey, misty monster thing out there! And it's coming this way!*

Now he was inside the ferry, not outside on the cold, blustery railing, he was less sure of what he'd seen. He was almost thirteen. He shouldn't be scared by misty grey islands and things that his tired brain likely made up.

It was probably nothing.

Probably.

A swirling mist-man with burning red eyes sniffed the air then slipped below the waves....

Myles gulped and looked at his sister on the other side of their sleeping mother.

"Bea!" he whispered.

She ignored him.

"Bea!" he said a little louder. She sighed and put a finger on her page. She lifted her eyes and raised her eyebrow in a silent, annoyed, *What?*

Myles wasn't sure what to say. He wanted to tell his sister, to tell someone about the *thing*, but what could he say? *There's* something *out there, in the water.*

"N — nothing," he stammered. The chance to tell someone was gone anyway since a moment later a voice came over the loudspeaker. Everybody jumped.

"Good evening, passengers, this is the captain speaking. We will be arriving in ten minutes. Please get ready to leave the ferry. If you are travelling by car, please go to your car now."

The loud voice woke his mother. She sat up and yawned.

"Are we there already? Myles, please hold Norman's hand." Then she shuffled around, gathering bags and Norman's toys. Bea stood up, but she never shifted her eyes from her book.

Myles held his little brother's hand and followed his mother and sister down the steep metal stairs to the bottom of the ferry. His foot clanged on the steps, echoing loudly in the belly of the ship. The belly of the beast.

There's a monster out there!

Just be calm. Breathe. You'll be off the ferry soon. It was nothing.

Probably.

Myles and his family found their car.

You should know a little about their car.

First of all, it was an ancient red Volvo.

Second, it was huge and roared like a dragon.

And third, Myles and his family named it Victor-the-Volvo, the enormous beast of a car. Unfortunately, Victor also stank. It smelled like every take-out meal they had eaten since they left home. There were wrappers and drink lids everywhere. Norman's peanut butter sandwiches were smeared all over the place. Plus, Norman had spilled a huge chocolate milk on the first day.

It was now clear to all of them that nothing gets out the stench of sour milk, no matter how hard you try to hide it. As he settled into his seat, Myles's stomach lurched again. He DID NOT want to add eau-de-barf to the car.

It was weird and a little creepy being at the bottom of the big ferry, waiting. It was dark down there, and you could hear the water slapping against the ship, just on the other side of Victor-the-Volvo's door. But now it was even worse.

Don't think about that thing in the water! Stop! You imagined it!

Myles's mother and Bea sat in the front. Norman was in his car seat in the back beside Myles, who tried to breathe normally and not focus on the stink of the car. He counted from one to ten then back down from ten to one a few times. He slowly curled and uncurled his fingers, then his toes.

Then Norman started singing.

"C, C, C, comes after B, B, B! But before D, D, D! Where we find C! C! C!"

Myles rolled his eyes and tried to tune it out. "Can't wait until he learns a new letter," he muttered. For the thousandth time, he wished he had something to listen to. But there was no money for electronics, or headphones, or anything like that. Except now, with his dad's new job, maybe there would be.

It didn't help him feel any better.

"… C! C! C! comes after B, B, B …!"

Finally, the ferry worker came along and told each driver, one by one, to start their car.

When it was their turn, Myles's mom turned the key.

Nothing happened.

She turned the key again. And again. And again.

And again.

It was no use.

Victor-the-Volvo, their trusty old car, wouldn't start.

Victor-the-Volvo was dead.

CHAPTER 3

GO HOME HIGHWAY

It's a bit of a problem, being stuck in the bottom of a ferry in a car that won't start. Every other car was stuck behind Myles and his family. People were frowning and pointing.

Myles dug down into his seat as far as he could.

The ferry man came with wires called "booster cables," and after what seemed like forever (but was probably only a few minutes), Victor roared back to life. The car wasn't dead anymore, but *everyone* on the ferry was looking at them. A girl in the next car stuck her tongue out at Myles.

Great, someone here hates me already.

At last, they left the ferry and joined a long line of cars turning onto the highway. Bea sat reading in the front seat, Norman sang to his teddy bear, a quieter song this time. Their mother drove and watched the road. It was all pretty normal. Myles was suddenly a little mad at himself for being scared by nothing.

Like a little kid.

The … thing … on the island was probably nothing.

It was misty out there … and cold. You were seeing things.

Myles looked out into the twilight. The fields were getting dark, and it looked like rain was coming. There were farmhouses dotting the highway, some with kitchen lights on. Some of them had children's swings outside or bikes propped against the kitchen door.

The car was almost peaceful for a while. It started to rain, and the windshield wipers clunked away.

Thunk-thunk, thunk-thunk.

Norman fell asleep and Myles reached across to tuck him under his Spiderman sleeping bag. His little brother looked so sweet: a four-year-old tyrant who also happened to look like an angel.

Myles looked out the window and his dad's voice popped into his head. Last night, when he spoke to his dad on his mother's cellphone, his dad said, "I can't wait to see you, and I have a surprise for you, Myles." But he wouldn't say what it was.

Myles hated surprises. Had his dad already forgotten that? What else had he forgotten about him? Myles frowned.

Then … it happened so suddenly.

A sign popped up beside the road. It said, GO HOME HIGHWAY, and Myles's mother veered toward it. She turned the car and they zoomed off the main highway, practically into a farmer's field. The car bumped along a rough dirt road.

"Mom! What are you doing?" Bea shouted. Their mom never turned sharp corners and they had driven halfway across the country without getting lost. No one wanted to get lost now.

What was she doing?

"Mom! This isn't the highway! The highway is over there, where all the other cars are!" Bea pointed at the line of red lights disappearing into the distance. The other cars from the ferry were moving away fast.

"Goodness!" their mother answered. "I must be getting sleepy. You're right, Bea. I have no idea why I turned off here. Just not paying attention, I guess."

"This isn't even a highway," Bea argued, sounding mad. She had done most of the map-reading so far, and they hadn't been lost once, a fact she mentioned constantly.

Until now.

Bea was right.

This was no highway. It was just a dirt road with trees hanging overhead. It was an abandoned dirt road too, judging by the potholes and bumps. Myles felt his stomach clench again.

He didn't want to be lost.

The sun was going down behind the rolling hills. The rain was falling a little harder.

Myles looked along the dirt road. Down at the end of the road he could see an old farmhouse. It looked abandoned and forgotten, and a light mist swirled around it in the coming dark. A huge black crow flew off the roof with a loud "CAW! CAW!" Myles got the feeling it didn't like to be disturbed. The whole place seemed like it didn't want to be disturbed.

Then ... *something* ran across the road between Myles and the farmhouse.

Something with RED EYES!

CHAPTER 4

CAW! CAW! CAUGHT!

Myles jumped. "What was *that*?" he yelled, pointing out the back window.

"What was what?" his mother asked, not looking. Myles peered again but there was nothing in the bushes. Nothing on the road.

"I ... I think there's ... *something* down there," Myles gulped. He couldn't bring himself to say *what*.

Myles's mother pulled over to the side of the dirt road. Victor roared and chugged like a dragon. She looked to where Myles had pointed, and squinted. "Where, Myles? I don't see anything. It's getting dark, though. Bea, please hand me the map." Bea reached into the glove box and handed her mother the old map. Once again, Myles wished they had one of those built-in computers that told you where you were and how to get where you wanted to go. He thought it might be called a GPS. Only *his* family would drive halfway across the country without one.

Maybe with his dad's new job, they could finally afford a new car. With a GPS.

While his mother tried to find "Go Home Highway" on the map, Myles struggled not to look down the dirt road again. He didn't want to see what was down at the end of the creepy road, but he couldn't help it. His imagination was running wild, which was much worse than not looking. He finally peeked.

No red eyes.

But the end of the road was swirling with mist, and the farmhouse looked really spooky and abandoned. The windows were all broken, and the front door swung and creaked in the rain.

Go Home Highway, what a joke! Myles thought. *More like Go Away Highway. Who would live here? Or ever want to?*

Suddenly he wondered what his old house looked like, now that no one lived in it. The house still wasn't sold when they left. Did it already look like this place, deserted and forgotten? How long did it take for a house to look unloved and unlived in, anyway?

And more than a little creepy?

And what was their new house like? What if it was terrible and lonesome, like this place?

Myles shuddered and peeked again at the abandoned farmhouse. The bushes along the dirt road definitely moved this time.

Something ran back across the road, closer to the car.

It looked right at Myles. RED EYES peered at him from the bushes!

He gulped.

"Mom! Get us out of here!" Myles whispered.

"What's gotten into you, Myles? Okay, you're right, 'Go Home Highway' was just a joke. It's not on the map. A big joke on me. I must want to get to Nobleville so badly that I wasn't paying attention." Myles's mother pulled the car around. Turning Victor-the-Volvo around wasn't easy. Victor was heavy and didn't exactly turn on a dime.

Myles's mother slowly turned the car, backed up, pulled forward, tried to miss the bushes at either side of the road ...

... then disaster. Victor-the-enormous got stuck in the mud!

"Great," their mother sighed. She got out of the car and looked at the back wheel. She whistled. Myles peeked over the back seat at her.

Please, please don't ask us to ...

"Get out of the car, you two! We aren't too stuck, I think we can get out of this mud with a little push."

Myles gulped. His heart started to pound. *The thing with red eyes* was out there!

Myles started to shake his head, but Bea teased him.

"Geesh, Myles, you look scared! Come on, the scariest thing out here is that crow, see?" She pointed at a giant crow above them in the trees. It was staring at them.

Myles dropped his gaze since he had the strangest feeling the crow wanted him to go away.

Nothing scared Bea, though. She pushed her glasses up her nose, put her precious book on the front seat, and left the car. Myles took a deep breath, opened his door, and stepped onto the pebbly, muddy dirt road. Light rain spattered down onto his head. It smelled like spring fields outside the car. The air was fresh and clean, a nice change from the inside of Victor.

But still. Myles's heart was pounding so hard, it hurt. He willed himself not to look down the road. At the farmhouse. Or at the bushes.

Stare at your feet! There's nothing out there!

He didn't want to see the door hanging on its hinges. The broken windows.

The *thing* from the island.

The huge black crow sat in the tree over-head, staring at them. Every now and then it ruffled its feathers.

"You both push hard, when I say. Okay?" His mother sounded so normal that Myles squeezed his eyes shut and nodded.

Bea put her back against the car and dug her feet into the dirt road. Myles put his hands on Victor's bumper, ready to push. He squeezed his eyes shut tighter.

"Ready?" their mother called from inside the car.

"Yes!" Bea shouted back, but Myles was mute.

"NOW!" their mother yelled. Victor roared. The back tire spun in the mud.

Bea and Myles pushed as hard as they could. Myles was SO glad his sister was there with him. There was no way he would be brave enough to stand in that creepy dirt road by himself. When Victor roared, the old crow in the tree let out a huge CAW! CAW!

It sounded like "Caught! Caught!" to Myles.

Bea and Myles pushed. The back tire spun, mud flew up at them, pebbles whipped past.

They pushed … and pushed … until Myles thought his arms were going to break. But suddenly the old car swerved back onto the gravel and out of the mud.

"Did it!" Bea said proudly.

But Myles couldn't rejoice. He couldn't speak. Behind her a pair of RED EYES stared out of the bushes.

A long, misty finger reached across the pebbly ground.

Myles tore into the car.

"Lock the doors! Come on, Mom! Let's go!"

"What's the matter with you, Myles? Would you mind if we wait until your sister gets into the car before we drive away?" she said calmly.

Bea strolled to the car. Slowly, far, far too slowly.

Myles couldn't yell at her to run. He was frozen. He wanted to scream at her to hurry up, but instead he squeezed his eyes shut and tucked his head into his collar.

Bea would have run if she'd seen the thing floating silently behind her along the road.

Long, misty grey arms reached out for her. A wispy grey face with a round, dark mouth opened wide. Red eyes danced and burned. The monster from the island drifted just behind her, sniffing the air and catching her scent.

Myles squeezed into a ball in the back seat beside sleeping Norman.

Bea settled into the front seat and shut the door. As his mother drove Victor-the-Volvo carefully down the lane back toward the highway, Myles had to look. It was much better to look than not to know. He peeked in the rear-view mirror, just for a second.

A sleek fox appeared in the lane behind the car. It stopped and stared at Myles in the gloom.

It has red eyes! Myles thought. *It was just a fox!*

"Hey, there's a fox!" he called, but it darted away into the ditch.

"Where? Where?" Bea asked, turning to see. "Sure ... a fox, right, Myles. Good one," she said, settling back into her seat, annoyed.

Myles was going to say, *No! It was really there!* but the words died in his throat. The fox was gone.

But it hardly mattered.

Because the monster from the island stood at the end of the road. It rose taller than the abandoned farmhouse. Two long grey arms stretched along the laneway toward Myles and the escaping car. The monster sniffed the air and two bright red eyes stared out of the gloom.

A dark, twisted mouth opened in the mist, and a whispery voice filled the air:

... I see you, Myles....

CHAPTER 5

DOG GONE WEIRD

myles stared straight ahead.

That wasn't a fox!

It was the THING, and I heard it! It spoke to me!

Myles watched the back of his mother's head as she drove. He saw the little light shining on Bea's open book. He heard rain on the car roof and the heavy wipers *thunk-thunking* across the windshield. Norman snored gently in his car seat.

Inside the car everything seemed normal.

But *outside*?

Myles gulped and stayed low in his seat. They were completely alone on the highway; all the other cars from the ferry were long gone. And it was raining harder now. They were going the right way again, but Myles had a terrible knot in his stomach.

The monster *followed* him from the ferry. It *hitched a ride*.

It spoke *to him*!

… I see you, Myles….

Myles could hear the horrible whispery voice perfectly. There was no doubt about it: the monster was outside the car. It had their scent. It was following them through the rainy fields.

Myles took four deep breaths, then two short breaths, then four deep ones again. He counted to ten, forward and backward. It helped, a little. But not enough. Not nearly enough.

He should tell someone.

"Mom?"

"Yes, Myles?" He bit his lip and looked outside. The fields were getting darker and darker. He wished he were brave.

Life would be so easy if he were brave. Like Bea. Or even Norman. He sighed.

"Mom? It's almost midnight. When are we going to get there?" The rain *splutted* against the windshield then fell just a little harder.

"Just go to sleep, Myles. Look, Norman's asleep. Bea is quietly reading. If you go to sleep, we'll be at our new house when you wake up. Dad will make us pancakes for breakfast. He can't wait to see us. And he's got a surprise for you, remember? Shhh."

But he should know I hate surprises!

Myles fidgeted and stared out the front window. He didn't want to turn his head a fraction. The white line of the highway darted past in the headlights, slick with rain. He needed to talk.

"When was the last time *you* slept, Mom? Like for real, a whole night, not just sitting upright on the ferry?"

His mother sighed. "I slept okay last night in the hotel."

Myles knew that was a lie. His mom had hardly slept at all since they left home. But he stayed silent. He thought about his dad making them pancakes, and about surprises. He thought about their new house.

What if our new house has broken windows and the front door is hanging off the hinges?

Myles scowled.

Bea sighed and said, "Look, Myles, just don't worry. I know you're worrying. Just relax."

Myles didn't answer them. They didn't know.

There was a monster outside.

Shapes moved along beside the car, the bushes and long grass beside the highway rustled with the wind. The rain made everything blurry. Myles closed his eyes. He tried to let the *thunk-thunk* of the wipers calm him. He talked to himself, trying to be brave.

There's nothing out there. You are too scared of everything. Mom is braver than you. Your sister is braver than you. Even your little brother is braver than you. Can't you be brave for once, too?

He took a deep breath and looked out the window.

And somehow didn't scream.

A huge grey figure strode across the muddy wet field. It loomed in the night sky, darker than the fields, drier than the rain. A creature of fog and air, mist and fear. Monster feet stomped across the cold April mud, keeping stride with the car. Blazing red eyes burned out of the darkness. Long, wispy arms reached out....

… I see you, Myles….

Myles gasped and clenched his eyes shut.

You're not there! You're not there!

"What's wrong?" his mother asked.

"Uh … uh … n … nothing." He squeezed his eyes tighter.

There's nothing out there!

"Mom, could you lock the doors?" he whispered.

Click. Click. Click. Click. The automatic "click" of four doors locking did nothing to calm him.

"You're awfully jumpy, Myles. You haven't been yourself since we left the ferry. What's wrong?" his mother asked quietly.

There's nothing out there.

Myles opened his eyes. He turned his head a fraction. Be brave, Myles! The field was empty.

See, nothing there. Maybe I should just tell her? he thought. His mother was always good at helping him feel calmer. But what would he say? *I saw a monster, Mom!* He was struggling to decide if he should tell her …

… when something jumped out of the ditch!

"MOM, WATCH OUT!" Myles shouted. It was a *dog*!

"There's a dog back there!"

Myles's mother slowed the car. "A dog? Where? Where, Myles?" she asked, slowing the car.

A large golden dog ran to Myles's side of the car. It might have been the reflection of the headlights, but the dog had a gentle glow about it. It looked at him then wagged its tail. It sniffed the air. The dog pricked up its ears at something in the field. Then it looked at Myles one last time and ran off into the darkness.

Myles turned in his seat to watch the dog through the rain. It was gone as quickly as it had arrived.

"I don't see a dog! Is this like the fox back there that no one else could see, Myles?" Bea snorted, twisting in her seat.

"I don't see it either, Myles, sorry," his mother said. "Are you sure you saw it? Are you sure it was a dog?"

"Yes, Mom. It was a big golden dog," Myles said, a little mad. Why hadn't his mother and sister seen the dog, too?

"Are you sure you didn't see it, Mom? It was right there!"

"No, I really didn't see it, Myles."

"There was no dog, was there, Myles?" Bea said flatly. She never had much patience for Myles's imagination. Or his worries.

"But it really was there, I didn't make it up!" Myles was getting upset. The dog was real. It sure *seemed* real. It had wagged its tail and pricked up its ears. It looked right at him then out into the field. But what if ... what if it wasn't really there?

No one saw the ... thing ... or the fox either. And now an invisible dog? Great, what if I'm cracking up?

Myles bit his lip. He didn't like the way this night was going at all. He closed his eyes and leaned back.

"Mom, can you please lock the doors?"

"They're locked, Myles."

"Can you please unlock them, and lock them again?"

Click. Click. Click. Click.

They were in the middle of absolutely nowhere, in the pitch black in the pouring rain.

Where had the dog come from? It had really seemed like it was trying to tell Myles something. It ran toward him and stared straight at him. Then it wagged its tail, sniffed the air.

Then it ran away. He wished his mother and Bea had seen it, too. That would definitely make him feel just a little better.

If you see that monster with the red eyes out there, dog, I hope you're braver than me!

CHAPTER 6

COURAGE

now Myles had more to worry about.

The monster was out there, calling his name. But a golden dog was out there, too. How did it get there? There were no farmhouses around. It was funny, but thinking about the dog helped Myles take his mind off the monster.

Bea put her book away, turned off her little book light, and closed her eyes. Their mother found a radio station and turned it down low. Although he didn't want it to, the whispery sound of country music lulled Myles. The *thunk-thunk, thunk-thunk* of the wipers made his eyes heavy.

He put his head against the window, determined not to sleep … and woke with a start.

He'd had a dream about the dog. It was running along beside the car, trying to tell him something. He sat up straight and wiped a little drool off his cheek.

Gross.

"Try to go back to sleep," his mother whispered. Myles sat up and looked at the clock on the dash. One forty-five. *In the morning.* He'd slept for almost an hour.

"Mom, can you turn up the heat? It's freezing in here." Cold rain pounded on the windshield. His mother turned the heat up high. Bea's head lolled gently against the window. He peeked over at Norman, who was snoring under his Spiderman sleeping bag. Norman's teddy bear stared at Myles with black plastic eyes.

Thunk-thunk, thunk-thunk.

The road stretched out ahead. Rain darted into the headlights.

Nothing. There is nothing out there. Just a dog.

And then …

… a man in a long coat loomed out of the darkness at the side of the road. He looked right at Myles.

"MOM! STOP! MOM!" His mother screeched on the brakes and pulled over to the side of the road.

"What! What is it now, Myles? Is it the dog again?" she asked, looking out the back window.

"There's a man over there." Myles pointed. His finger shook. There WAS a man standing at the side of the road, no denying it this time. He was bathed in an eerie glow from the red lights of the car.

"You see him, right?" Myles asked, suddenly worried.

"Yes, I see him," his mother said. She peered out the back window a moment longer then moved to open the door.

"Mom! No!" Myles tried to stop her. *Don't go outside! The monster is out there!*

"Whuss going on?" Bea asked, mumbly from sleep.

"There's a man over there!" Myles pointed.

Bea rubbed her eyes and adjusted her glasses. "Is this another of your fantasies, Myles?"

"NO! He's right there!" Myles said loudly. *Please see him, Bea!*

His mom went to open the door again, and Myles leaned over and grabbed her arm.

"Mom! Don't go out there! Please!"

"Myles, what's gotten in to you? A lost dog that no one but you saw is one thing, a person lost out here in the rain and the dark is another." His mother opened the door and stepped onto the road. The cold air and rain blew into the car like a cloud.

Myles looked at Bea and shook his head.

"Don't go out there!" he pleaded, but Bea just laughed.

"Gee, little brother, it's just a guy. Come on, if you're so worried, you can help protect us." Bea opened her door and stepped out into the darkness.

Myles took a peek at Norman, who was fast asleep. He had no choice but to follow his mother and sister outside. He opened his door and cautiously walked to the back of the car. He DID NOT look toward the fields all around them; instead he kept his eyes down. Rain spluttered onto their uncovered heads while Victor roared and chugged behind them.

There's nothing out there! Just look at your feet!

The man stood, half-hidden in darkness beside the black fields. He wore a long, dark coat and a bright red scarf. The rain fell onto his peaked hat.

"Hello, sir?" Myles's mother called. Bea and Myles stood beside her. It was raining harder and a little windy now, so Myles wasn't sure if the man heard them.

But he did. Very slowly the man turned and smiled at them. He was elderly, with a white moustache.

He started to walk toward them. It was weird, but Myles thought he looked almost like he was ... floating. He wondered if the man was a ballet dancer when he was younger. He was the most graceful old person he'd ever seen.

"Sir, are you okay?" Myles's mother called into the dark, but the man didn't answer them.

"Sir! Do you need help? Are you lost?" Myles's mother took her phone out of her pocket and held it up. "I have a phone! Do you need me to call for help?" But again he didn't answer.

He moved toward them along the dark, wet pavement. The rain spattered onto his

raincoat and his rich leather shoes. Myles noticed the man didn't look soaking wet, not as wet as he should. Maybe he hadn't been out there very long?

Myles moved closer to his mother. Bea moved closer to Myles and took his hand. He squeezed her hand back.

This was creepy. The man walked closer, close enough for them to see his face. He grinned, and Myles drew back. The man's eyes looked strange, glowing red from the lights of the car.

Then the man spoke in a funny, faraway voice. "Thank you for stopping! I'm afraid I've lost my dog. Have you seen him?"

Dog?

Myles felt his heart slow down a little. Maybe he was just a nice old man looking for his dog?

Out for a walk in the middle of nowhere, in the pouring rain, at two o'clock in the morning?

The man smiled again. It was an odd smile, like it didn't get an outing very often. Now that he was closer, Myles thought the man looked weird. Out of place. His coat, his shoes, even his hat all seemed wrong somehow. His mother answered.

"A dog? Why, yes! Yes! We did see a dog. Well, I didn't, but my son saw a dog, about an hour ago." She sounded relieved. "Right, Myles?"

"Y-yes … it was golden," Myles answered. "A big golden dog." He wanted to add, *he was glowing, and he pricked up his ears and wagged his tail at me*, but he didn't. For some reason that seemed like it was private, just for him.

"Yes, that's him! Was he okay?" the strange man called back. There was definitely something wrong with his voice. He sounded too far away, like he was talking to them through a door.

Maybe it's the wind?

Myles shrugged. "He seemed okay, I didn't see him for long," he called out.

The old man nodded and turned away. "I'm sure I'll find him, then! Sorry to have troubled you," he said.

"I'd love to help you look for him, but I'm afraid my children and I are in a hurry," his mother called out into the rain.

"Oh, no need. I'll keep looking for him myself. If you saw him, I'm sure I'll find him any minute now." The old man turned to head back down the highway.

Myles's mother hesitated. The rain suddenly fell a little harder. The cold April wind whipped into their faces.

"Sir! It's two o'clock in the morning, and pouring rain! Are you sure you don't want me to drop you off back at home? You can look for your dog tomorrow?" She was shouting into the darkness now. The man had almost disappeared down the highway.

Myles could tell his mother didn't really want to pick up a stranger. She didn't really want to make room in the back seat between him and Norman for this old man. But there was something about him that seemed lost.

Very, very lost.

The man stopped and turned back to look at them. He didn't smile this time.

"Oh no, I'm afraid I have to find my dog tonight. He's very precious, you see. His name is Courage. He is always there when I need him, I can't lose him now. I don't want to trouble you, madam. You and your children look like you've driven a long way. You just get back into your automobile and head along. If you want, you could tell them at the next gas depot that you saw Pete Fournette out looking for his lost dog. They'll know what to do."

Gas depot? Does that mean gas station?

Myles's mother nodded. "Okay, if you're sure you don't want a ride? Okay, we'll do that. We'll stop at the next gas depot … station … and tell them Pete Fournette is looking for his dog. Courage. Take care. Be careful!" Myles's mother shouted that last sentence at the old man's retreating back.

He raised his leather-gloved hand in a backward wave. Then he disappeared over the ditch into the dark field.

"Mom, that was weird," Myles whispered. Bea was still holding his hand. He didn't even mind.

His mother nodded as they got back into the car. At the sound of the door, Norman mumbled, "Whazzz happnin'?" but he didn't wake up. He drifted back to sleep, clutching his teddy bear and his truck.

Myles did NOT want Norman to wake up. Not now. He couldn't handle loud singing about the letter C! C! C! at the moment. Or any seat-kicking. Plus, if Norman woke up, he'd most likely have to pee, and who knew how long that would take? Myles just wanted to get out of there.

"Yeah, weird is definitely the word for what that was. We'll stop at the next gas station and tell them." Myles's mother pulled Victor back onto the empty highway.

Click. Click. Click. Click.

For the first time in four days, Myles's mother locked all the car doors and he didn't even have to ask.

CHAPTER 7

MYSTERY ON THE WALL

Myles tried to relax, but he couldn't. The rain, the darkness, the dog, the man ...

... the monster out there ...

His eyes flickered to the car window and the dark, misty fields beyond.

What was the old man doing out in the middle of nowhere, at two o'clock in the morning, looking for his dog?

In the *rain*?

It must be a really special dog. And what if the old man saw *red eyes* out there? Myles shuddered. As spooky and weird as the old man was, he couldn't wish the red-eyed monster on him.

Bea was fast sleep. Norman, too. Myles knew he was never going to sleep, possibly ever again. He shifted around in his seat. He stared at the ceiling.

Then he blurted out, "Mom ... do you think that old man will find his dog?"

"I don't know, Myles. You saw the dog ... I don't see why not." She answered in a distant voice, which meant she wasn't really listening.

"Well," Myles went on, "how do you think the old man got onto the road? He wasn't wet and he had no car...." He trailed off.

But his mother wasn't in the mood for talking. "Not now, Myles, please," she begged. She shushed him and put the radio on low. Myles closed his eyes.

I sure hope that dog is okay. And the old man. I hope they find each other.

It was getting crowded with things to worry about outside the car.

The wipers *thunk-thunked*, the rain pattered against the glass, the radio crackled and hissed ... then Myles woke with a jolt. When did he fall asleep? His mom was pulling

Victor-the-Volvo into an all-night gas station and diner. The car slowed down, and the tires rumbled on the soft gravel. It was bright, too bright. The neon lights above the gas pumps were glaring and weird after all the darkness of the road and the empty fields.

A sign beside the gas pump said, "Welcome to Fleshington."

Fleshington? What kind of creepy name is that for a town? Whose flesh?

Myles rubbed his eyes and looked over at the car clock: 2:31 a.m. He was only asleep for fifteen minutes. Would this stupid night never end? He was beginning to think that Nobleville didn't really exist and they were on some endless drive in a scary movie. The kind where no one ever gets anywhere, and it's always nighttime. And raining.

... with a monster outside ... stop it!

His mom parked in front of the tiny restaurant next to the gas station and turned off the engine. Victor rattled and sighed to silence. The sudden quiet hurt Myles's head.

"Mom, are you sure that was smart? Turning off Victor? What if he doesn't start again?" Myles asked. Bea stretched and yawned.

"We're in a gas station, Myles. They fix cars here. If Victor won't start after we eat, then we wait a few hours until the sun comes up and the mechanic comes to work. No problem." She sounded tired.

"I need a cup of coffee. The car needs some gas. Since you're both awake, we might as well eat something, too." Myles's mother and sister opened their doors and stepped outside. Cold, clean air hit him inside the car like a slap. He took a deep breath. He'd almost gotten used to the stink of chocolate milk, peanut butter, and eau-de-Norman.

Myles didn't want to move. He really didn't. But he could see that he had no choice. He took a deep breath, opened his door, and joined his mother and sister. He tried not to look across the road into the dark fields. He didn't need any red eyes or voices in his head, thank you.

But nothing happened. The rain fell lightly. The bright light from the restaurant sign hurt his eyes. His mom undid Norman's seatbelt and slung him over her shoulder like a tired sack of potatoes. Norman didn't even wake up.

Norman's truck smashed onto the gravel at their feet. Myles stared at it for moment then picked it up and tossed it into the back seat with Norman's bear.

A pickup truck pulled into the station as their mother locked the car.

"SQUAWK! Cluck, cluck, cluck." There were dozens of chickens in the back of the truck, huddled against the cold and rain. A man got out of the truck and walked into the diner ahead of them.

The wet chickens squawked.

Glad I'm not a chicken!

Bea, Myles, his mother, and his sack-of-potatoes-brother entered the diner. It was old and well used. A slow fan whirled around the ceiling. Every table or counter was either chipped or sticky with coffee cake crumbs.

Classy it was not.

It might have been the weird greenish light. It might have been the fact that it was two thirty in the morning. Or it might have been because he was *seeing things* outside, but Myles thought the place looked unfriendly.

The man from the chicken truck sat at the counter. The waitress went over and took his order. Myles's mom plopped Norman into a corner booth like a ragdoll. Norman still didn't wake up. Myles had a pang of jealousy. He suddenly wished HE was four years old, too — then maybe none of this stupid horrible car trip would matter. He could sleep through the whole thing like Norman.

His mom slid in next to Norman and took off her coat. Bea pushed in beside Myles. Everyone looked tired and grumpy. Except Norman, of course, he just looked like an angel.

Myles was suddenly worried at how they must look. His mom was bleary and mussed up. Norman was covered in smeared peanut butter. Bea was pale and her eyes looked huge and bug-like under her glasses. Myles didn't even want to know what he looked like. A beast of some sort, with red eyes.

Stop!

No wonder the Chicken Truck Man and the waitress kept glancing over at them. Myles and his family were hideous.

The waitress walked over to their booth. She was wearing brightly coloured clothes. She was *too* bright. She made Myles nervous.

"Hi! What can I get you folks?" she said too loudly, then popped her chewing gum.

Weird. Who chews gum at two thirty in the morning? Myles thought.

Myles's mom looked up and smiled weakly. "Yes, sorry, we must look dreadful. We've been driving all night off the ferry. We've actually been on the road for four days, and we're trying to make it to our new house before morning." She smiled again, trying to be polite.

"Oh, you folks must be tired! You need some coffee, right away!" The waitress popped her gum and twirled around. She was too happy, too full of energy, to be real. Myles laid his head on the table. Odd how he couldn't sleep in the car, but he felt like he could sleep in the diner just fine. The waitress came back and poured their mother a cup of coffee.

"Now, what can I getcha?" she smiled.

"A grilled cheese sandwich and fries for me, please." His mother yawned. Myles ordered the same thing. So did Bea.

No one spoke. When the food came, Myles, his sister, and mother ate in total silence, staring straight ahead. Norman slept on. The rain grew louder. It poured onto the pavement outside the diner as the little fan turned slowly above their heads. Outside, the wet chickens squawked in the back of their truck.

As Myles ate, he couldn't shake the feeling that everything outside the car was connected. There was something terrible following them, he knew it. There was a lost dog and a wandering old man with nowhere to be out there, too. And now miserable chickens.

What was real? What wasn't? Myles was too tired to know the difference.

The only thing he DID know is that he wanted to BE somewhere. But where? He didn't want to be in Nobleville — that wasn't home. He really just wanted to go back to his *real* home. His old home. But that was impossible.

Where *was* home now? What was it going to be like if they finally got there?

He suddenly wasn't very hungry. He pushed his plate away.

"Mom, I'm going to the bathroom," he said. He climbed over Bea and slid out of the booth. He needed some space, somewhere away from his family for a few minutes. He wandered along a dark, cramped hallway to the bathroom. He didn't really have to go.

Instead, he looked at himself in the cracked little bathroom mirror.

He looked bad. His hair was plastered to his face. His skin was green ... was it the light? He stuck his tongue out ... and even his tongue looked weird.

What's wrong with me? I look like a monster, all I need are red eyes!

STOP IT! You have to get a grip on yourself. Go and finish your food.

On his way back to the booth, Myles stopped. And stared. An old picture hung on the wall. Myles got closer and peered.

He rubbed his eyes.

He stood in front of the picture and stared harder. It was old. It was so old that you almost couldn't see the black-and-white image because it was so faded. Myles put his face right up to the picture. The frame was greasy with age, but if you looked hard enough you could see the photograph: an old man with a moustache and a scarf sat in an old-fashioned car. Beside him sat a beautiful dog. Underneath were the words, "Pete Fournette and his dog, Courage."

"It's *them*!" Myles whispered.

He let his eyes drift further down the photograph. At the very bottom was a faint pencilled date: April 1908.

Over one hundred years ago.

CHAPTER 8

THE BALLAD
OF PETE FOURNETTE

Myles looked over at his family in the booth. The Chicken Truck Man sat nearby, quietly sipping coffee. The waitress hummed over the coffee pot, wiping glasses.

It all seemed pretty normal. Or at least what passed as normal on this weird night.

But there was nothing normal about the photograph on the wall.

What were Pete Fournette and his dog doing in a one-hundred-year-old photograph?

It didn't make any sense. Pete Fournette was wearing the peaked hat, the silk scarf, even the leather gloves that Myles just saw him wearing back on the road. Myles backed away from the picture. He backed up toward the booth until he slowly sat down beside his sister. Bea glanced up at him and did a double-take.

"What's the matter with *you*? You look like you've seen a ghost!"

Myles shook his head. "I'm … I'm really not sure," he answered. "There's a picture, with a dog … over there…."

"Oh!" Myles's mother suddenly came to life. "Thanks for reminding me, Myles! I'm so tired, I almost forgot! Waitress! Excuse me!" she called. She lifted her hand, and the waitress hurried over with the coffee pot.

"More coffee?" the waitress asked, smiling and chewing her gum.

"I almost forgot to tell you!" Myles's mother said. "We met a man, back on the road. An old man, looking for his dog."

There's a picture of him on the wall, Myles wanted to add, but didn't.

"I didn't actually see the dog, but my son did. What was his name, again?"

"Courage," Myles said, not looking up.

"Yes, Courage, that's right. Then a little further down the road, an old man stopped us and asked if we'd seen the dog. And the old man's name was …"

"Pete Fournette?" the waitress answered in a whisper. Her face was white. She placed the coffee pot on the table then sat down hard. Myles had the feeling she had to sit down suddenly. It was either sit down or fall down.

"Yes, that's right. You know him?" Myles's mother asked.

The lady nodded and whistled softly through her teeth. "That's a name I haven't heard in a while … a LONG while. It's a name I thought I wouldn't hear again, to tell you the truth." She looked slowly at each of them. Then she took a deep breath.

"What is it?" Myles's mother searched the waitress's face. The waitress looked uncomfortable and shifted her weight on the creaky old seat.

"Well, it's like this …" but she hesitated.

"Just tell them, Loretta!" the Chicken Truck Man at the counter said so loudly that everyone jumped.

"Tell us what?" Myles's mother looked

a little worried now. The waitress, Loretta, looked nervous. "Well …"

Clearly, there was something *very wrong* with Pete Fournette.

Mr. Chicken Truck Man got up and walked over to the booth. He wore a broken old baseball cap and greasy overalls. He leaned into their faces and whispered, "What Loretta here doesn't want to tell you is, there IS no Pete Fournette. Not strictly speaking. That old coot and his dog have been dead for over one hundred years."

Dead? DEAD? One hundred years?

Myles's mother blinked at Mr. Chicken Truck Man. "What? What … what does THAT mean? He's not dead, he's out there looking for his dog."

But Myles slowly knew what Mr. Chicken Truck Man meant. He couldn't bring himself to say it … but he knew all the same.

April 1908. It made perfect sense. Or was starting to.

Loretta drew in close to them. Just as though on cue, a flash of lightning lit up the rain outside the diner, followed by a boom of thunder. It was almost theatrically spooky. Myles gulped.

"This old diner used to be a roadhouse," Loretta said. "It was the first and oldest gas station on this part of the highway. Well, back then they called it a gas depot. It's been here a long, long time. Pete and his dog used to go for a Sunday drive and come in here all the time." Loretta paused. The family stared at the waitress.

Mr. Chicken Truck Man finished the story for her. "Now Pete Fournette comes out on rainy nights at this time of year. He stops lonely travellers and asks for help finding his dog," he said, just to make sure they got the point.

"No one has ever seen his dog, though. I've never heard of that before," Loretta added thoughtfully, looking at Myles.

"Well, what do you mean?" Myles's mother was shaking her head back and forth, like the words just didn't make any sense.

And they didn't. They just didn't. Except they really kind of did.

"Pete Fournette and his dog are dead, Mom. These people are saying that they're *ghosts*," Bea piped up. Myles was suddenly thankful that his sister was so logical about everything. Saying it out loud made it sound crazy … but true.

It had to be true. What else would explain the gentle glowing of the dog, or how odd the old man looked? How faraway his voice sounded? Or how he was so out of place, and not wet in the rain? Or the picture from 1908?

It all made perfect sense to Myles.

"Bea's right. They're *ghosts*, Mom," he said, quietly.

"*Ghosts?*" His mother was doing an excellent impression of someone who just couldn't make sense of what she was being told. As though Mr. Chicken Truck Man and Loretta had just told her that she was living on Mars, or that she was about to sprout a second head.

"How can they be … *ghosts?*"

Myles knew he had to tell her. He drew up his courage and blurted it out. "There's a really old picture over there on the wall, Mom. It's Pete Fournette and his dog. It says April 1908 on the bottom." Myles pointed at the picture in the hallway, but his mother just stared at him. Now he felt like maybe he should have kept that fact to himself. He suddenly felt a tiny bit sorry for his mother. The look on her face was a strange mixture of horror and exhaustion. She looked like she might just burst into crazy laughter at any second.

Myles didn't think he could handle that.

Luckily, Loretta finished the story, speaking quickly. "Pete Fournette was a rich old man who lived around here. One rainy spring night in 1912, his beloved dog, Courage, ran off. Old Pete went out to find him. He was walking beside the highway, then ... he disappeared. No one ever saw him again, although they looked and looked. His dog came home the next day, just fine."

"So why did I see the dog, too?" Myles asked.

"I don't know, like I said, that's a first," Loretta said quietly.

"So, we just saw ... a *ghost*?" Myles's mother was finally catching on.

Mr. Chicken Truck Man and Loretta both nodded silently. Then Loretta got up and walked through the swinging doors into the kitchen. They heard her rattle around for a few moments, then she walked back out holding an old book. She blew dust off the cover then sat down in the booth.

"I know it's weird. But people do see old Pete's ghost now and then. This is a log of all the people who have seen Pete over the years." Loretta opened it, and Myles, Bea, and his mother all crowded forward to look at the pages. There were names and dates on each page, and signatures of people.

James McReady of Tottenham swears right and true that he saw old Pete Fournette walking the highway on this rainy night, April 4th, 1914 ...

Evelyn Williams and her daughter Kate, of Wickhurst, saw old Pete Fournette on this rainy night, April 18th, 1916 ...

Jane, Efrieda, and Benjamin Norland of Hillsburgh, saw and talked to old Pete Fournette plain and clear on this rainy night of April 7th, 1918. (Pete was offered a ride in the wagon, but refused it and strode off into the night.)

On and on the entries went. Bea was fascinated and read slowly through all the pages. Myles had enough after Jane, Efrieda, and Benjamin Norland of Hillsburgh. He got the picture.

Pete and his dog Courage were long dead.

And somehow *he* had seen them both.

Myles noticed that his mother had stopped reading, too. Instead she was drumming her nails on the table, a bad habit when she was nervous. Loretta spoke up.

"This is just our old log. If the local library was open down the highway, you could go ask Mrs. Cody, the librarian, to show you the archives. They're more accurate and have photos and more information. Mrs. Cody tells the story of Pete Fournette on her summer ghost walks. The local kids all know the story off by heart ... he's a pretty well-known ghost around here. We used to get people in here all the time saying they saw him. Not so many lately, though. You're the first in a while."

"The last entry was 1998, to be exact," Bea piped up. She'd finished reading the log-book and was pointing at the last page.

Joe & Tara Donne, Toronto, April 2nd, 1998. Driving in the rain with the kids, when out of the blue a man appears. We slammed on the brakes. The man asked if we saw his dog and floated away over the fields ...

"There are almost fifty entries in here," Bea said.

"It's fifty-two, actually," Loretta nodded. Myles's mother didn't budge. She was staring into the middle distance, clutching her coffee cup.

Myles felt a shiver deep inside. He KNEW something was wrong with that old man.

But Courage? Courage seemed more real, somehow.

"If you want to know more, check with Mrs. Cody. Tomorrow. At the library," Loretta said helpfully. "She'll want to take your pictures for the archives and get your full names and more information."

"No thanks, we've seen enough," their mother said quietly. "We really just want to go home."

"Can you sign our logbook?" Loretta asked brightly.

"No, sorry. We've got to get going. Just say ..." Myles's mother looked at her children for a moment. "Just say that a very tired family on a long, long drive saw Pete Fournette tonight."

"And his dog," Myles added quickly.

His mother nodded and said wearily, "Yes, and his dog." Then she paid their bill, gathered up sack-of-potatoes Norman, and they left.

When the door slammed behind Myles and his family, Mr. Chicken Truck Man sighed.

"I gotta get those chickens to the farm, Loretta. I'm late. But I wonder ... I wonder if old Pete will ever find peace?"

Loretta looked sadly out the window into the rainy night. "I hope so, but he's a restless ghost. He's been around a long time."

She hesitated. "Still, they saw the dog. Maybe that counts for something. Maybe this time Pete will find what he's looking for," she whispered.

The Chicken Truck Man paid his bill and left. Loretta stared after him, looking out at the rainy night for a long while. She had written one word in the book where Myles's family name should have been: *Courage*.

CHAPTER 9

CHICKEN ALL OVER

yles, Bea, sleeping Norman, and their mother all sat in the car. In a fit of sisterly love, Bea had told Myles he could sit in the front seat. Within seconds he remembered that the back seat was roomier, which was probably why Bea wanted it.

Before she started the engine, Myles's mother cleared her throat. She had something to say.

"Myles, Bea, I don't want to talk about what just happened. In the diner. About the ... about Pete Fournette and his dog. We can talk about it, maybe even laugh about it one day years from now. But not tonight. Right now, I have to get us home."

Bea laughed. "I don't know what you're so worried about, Mom! It's just a trick. Come on, you don't *really* think that Pete and his dog are *ghosts*, do you? Frankly, I think they just plant the dog and the spooky old guy out on the highway at this time of year. When someone stops to help, 'Pete' sends them to the diner so Loretta can sell more coffee and grilled cheese sandwiches."

"What about the log book?" their mother asked.

"Fake, obviously," Bea said. She sounded so sure.

"What about the old picture? On the wall?" Myles asked.

"Fake. All fake."

"But why? Why would they fake it, Bea?" their mother asked. She sounded like she really, really wanted to be convinced by Bea.

Bea shrugged. "For fun? Because they're bored? To make money on tourists in the slow season? Who knows? Goodnight!" Then she laid her head on the back seat next to Norman and within a few moments she was snoring.

It was so unfair. Why did Bea and Norman get to sleep through everything? And trust Bea to come up with a completely sane explanation for a ghost. *Ghosts.*

But Myles and Bea were very different; they never agreed on anything. The old man was so strange, Myles knew there was something ghostly about him. And the dog *was* glowing, although there was no point telling anyone since no one would believe him. And the old photograph on the wall was no fake, he was sure of it.

Myles tried hard not to think about what just happened, but he couldn't help it. Bea was wrong. He had a sneaking suspicion his mother didn't believe Bea's explanation, either. Although she might have wanted to.

I don't care what Bea says, that old man was a ghost.

Myles's mother turned the key in the ignition.

Nothing happened.

That beautiful dog was a ghost, too. Courage.

She turned the key again.

Nothing happened.

She turned the key one more time and pumped the gas pedal.

But even if they are ghosts, the dog and the old man aren't nearly as scary as the monster out there.

Victor roared to life, with thick black smoke chugging out the back. They rolled away from the diner. Rain hit the top of the car and ran in streams down the windows. A little water leaked in through the back window, it was raining so hard. But then the back window always leaked, a little. The wipers *thunk-thunked* across the windshield, barely clearing a path through the water. Once in a while, the deep hum of thunder rolled over the fields.

Myles's mother drove very slowly. Too slowly. She drove like someone who was just learning to drive. She gripped the wheel so tightly that Myles could see her white knuckles.

His mom was nervous. She was a good driver, but Myles had never seen her so tense. He suddenly longed for some help.

"Mom, let's call Dad." It came out of the blue. Myles was mad at his dad, it was true. They were only in this mess because of him. For making them move across the country. But still, it might help to hear Dad's voice. It might make everything seem … more real.

"Oh, Myles, I'd love to call him, but it's three in the morning," his mother answered. "He's asleep anyway. I don't want to bother him when we're so close. I want to surprise him. Plus, my phone is almost dead. I've only got one more phone call left before it dies for good."

Myles frowned then pushed that thought away. Wait. His dad didn't *deserve* a phone call.

"Mom, can you lock the doors, please?"

Click. Click. Click. Click.

He thought about the weird night. On the plus side, he hadn't seen or heard the monster for several hours. Not since before he saw Courage. Maybe it had stopped following them. Maybe it was gone. Myles bit his lip.

Maybe.

Headlights caught up to them. Mr. Chicken Truck Man and his soaked birds pulled past. He waved as he drove by. Water from his tires sprayed all over the windshield, and Myles's mother cursed under her breath.

Then the red lights of the chicken truck disappeared down the road. Mr. Chicken Truck Man had driven by fast, very, very fast.

Victor-the-Volvo rolled along for a while, very slowly. Myles was determined not to look out into the fields. He gave up checking the time. It didn't matter anymore. Nothing mattered. Nobleville didn't really exist, and they'd never get out of the car. They'd drive on this highway forever....

Myles woke with a start. The car was slowing down, skidding in the rain.

Then … lights.

There were red lights gleaming on the road up ahead. People stood at the side of the highway in the pouring rain. Victor-the-Volvo skidded to a stop.

"What now?" Myles's mother said under her breath.

A workman in a huge, flapping, yellow rain poncho and a hardhat stood in the middle of the road. Flares lit up the road ahead of him. Myles could see the flashing lights of a police car. His mother lowered the car window, water lashing into her eyes. A huge boom of thunder rolled over the car. She looked up into the workman's face.

"What's the problem?" She had to yell to be heard over the rain and wind.

The workman leaned into the car. Rain smacked across his face and dripped off the end of his nose.

"Bad accident up ahead, ma'am, sorry. You'll have to take a detour," he yelled.

Myles's mother blinked. "A *detour*? Why?" she yelled back. At that very moment a red-eyed chicken strutted by on the road. The chicken looked at Myles, ruffled its feathers, and walked on.

"The highway is closed up ahead. A farm truck overturned. There are chickens running all over the road, all over the field."

Another wet chicken blew by the outside of the car and tumbled along the road. It blew on past, caught up in the wind. It had weird red eyes, glowing in the reflection of the car lights. More soaking, red-eyed chickens followed. They looked like tumbleweeds. A few of them flapped or strutted as they blew past the car.

Myles rubbed his own eyes, which he was sure were red and bleary-looking, too.

Tumble-chickens? What can possibly happen next?

His mother was still yelling at the man in the poncho.

"Couldn't we just drive on past? If we were careful?" Myles had never heard his mother's voice sound like that before. Angry? Annoyed? Fed up?

Desperate?

"Sorry, ma'am. Everything is taped off, there's no way to get past. But the detour will take you through those hills over there." The man pointed at a far-off forest on a hill. The trees looked dark and frightening. Myles got an instant chill down his back.

"Just drive until you see the red detour sign, then turn left. It'll take you fifteen minutes out of your way. Sorry." The workman spread his soggy hands and shrugged. He was trying to be nice. A policewoman came over to the car.

"Move along, ma'am," she said. She didn't have a flapping rain poncho like the workman, and she looked soaked to the bone.

"Is the driver okay?" Myles's mother shouted at the policewoman.

"He's okay, not making much sense though. Talking about red eyes, red eyes. You've got to move along now, ma'am," the policewoman answered.

Myles froze.

RED EYES?

Myles's mother nodded. She couldn't exactly argue with a police officer. She rolled up her window and brushed back her wet hair.

Myles peeked at the wrecked chicken truck blocking the road. His stomach lurched.

"Mom, I think ... I think the chicken truck crashed because of me!" It *must* have been his fault. The policewoman said *red eyes*. Mr. Chicken Truck Man must have seen ... *the monster*!

"What's gotten in to you, Myles? Of course it's not your fault. It's just an accident." His mother looked over at him.

"No, Mom, there's something out there, something following us!" Myles was too upset to say any more, but it did feel better to finally tell his mother a little about what was bothering him.

She didn't understand.

"Myles, the ghost story was weird, okay. Even if Bea is right, even if it was just a trick, it's a pretty scary one. I understand, you're a little anxious. More anxious than normal, maybe. But you didn't cause the accident. There's nothing following us, or I would have seen it. Look, Bea and Norman are sleeping. Just go to sleep. I'll get us there, I promise. Dad's pancakes for breakfast, remember?" She smiled at Myles and put her hand on his. "It'll be okay, we'll take the detour and get back on the highway before you know it. Go to sleep."

Myles's stomach was a giant knot. There was NO WAY he was going to sleep. Not now. The car started very slowly down the bumpy gravel road.

They were on the detour.

Myles had thought it was dark on the highway, but the back roads were even darker, if that was possible. The trees were too close to the road, and he couldn't see very far ahead or behind the car. It started to rain harder than ever, the wind picked up, thunder rolled, low and ominous. Myles's mom turned the wipers up high. They made a horrible shriek, so she had to turn them back down to the medium setting, the *thunk-thunk* setting.

The detour road wasn't smooth like the highway. It was bumpy gravel, rock, and mud. The road turned to muddy guck beneath the car wheels. He and his mom peered out the car windshield together, into the endless night.

"M — Mom? Can you see anything?" Myles asked quietly.

His mom nodded. "Yes, if I go slowly enough, I can see the road. Don't worry. Check on Bea and Norman for me?"

Myles turned around, and there were his brother and sister, fast asleep. Bea's glasses were crushed into her cheek, and Norman looked like a little angel. Their heads were touching, and Bea had her arm across Norman's knees.

Myles was hit with a pang of worry for his sister and his little brother. They looked so helpless. He wanted to protect them from this rotten night.

Ghosts were one thing. Bea and his mother didn't seem too worried about *them*.

Monsters were another. He was the only one who *knew* the truth, knew for sure what was following them, so he was the only one who could protect them.

Suddenly, he was glad his brother and sister were asleep. If he couldn't sleep, at least he could help his mother watch over them. It would be his job to keep them safe.

Then Myles had a terrible thought.

Norman *MUST NOT* wake up. If he did, that would mean he'd have to pee. And if he had to pee, they'd have to stop. And the last thing Myles wanted was to stop on that scary back road.

But sometimes, when something suddenly occurs to you, it's because a part of you knows it's about to happen.

Myles held his breath ... *don't wake up, Norman!*

But Norman's blue eyes slowly flickered open. He looked at Myles and then opened his eyes wide.

"Haz to pee," Norman whispered.

CHAPTER 10

NORMAN HAZ TO GO

norman had been asleep for hours.

He'd slept through Go Home Highway, two ghosts, and a creepy diner.

And a monster.

He'd slept through a rainy night and a truck crash, but NOW that they were in the middle of nowhere on the scariest road imaginable … he had to wake up and PEE?

Myles looked at his mom. No doubt about it this time, she looked worried.

"Um, Norman. Could you please hold it?" she asked quietly.

"PEE!"

One thing Myles, Bea, and their mother did *not* take for granted was Norman's bladder. There was no knowing when it was going to make itself part of the immediate needs of the family. There was no taming it.

"Mom! I *told* you we should have made him wear a pull-up!" Myles's mother shot him a "that's enough" look. The one thing that would make Norman fight them like a Bengal tiger was the word "pull-up." Myles shut up.

"Okay, Norman, we'll stop. In. A. Minute."

Norman booted the back of Myles's seat. Again, again, and again. He was going to pee right then and there, and then the car wouldn't just reek of chocolate milk and peanut butter anymore.

"PEE! PEE! PEE!"

Myles and his mother exchanged a look, then his mother pulled the car to the side of the road. It was not like anyone was going to come down this dark, deserted, terrifying alley of blackness, ever.

Except to find their bodies one day.

STOP! Stop thinking scary, crazy things!

Myles willed himself not to think.

They were going to have to GO OUTSIDE.

"Okay, Norman. I'm getting you out of the car. You can go pee." Their mother said this very quietly and evenly, like she was bargaining with a madman.

Pleading with Norman and his pee.

"Myles, you can stay here with Bea," she said evenly. But there was no way Myles was letting his mother and little brother go out there alone.

It was out there.

"No, Mom, I'll come. I can keep watch." His mother looked at him oddly but didn't argue.

Then, like a well-timed machine, Myles and his mother both opened their doors. Rain lashed into Myles's face. The smell of pine trees and farmland slapped him wide awake. And it was cold. Suddenly much, much colder than it had seemed when they got into the car at the diner. The constant whine of wind through the trees filled his ears, and Victor's roar drowned out their voices. On cue, there was another theatrical roll of thunder.

Myles wrapped his arms around himself and counted to ten, then to twenty, then back down to zero. He focused on the tip of his shoe in the mud, on the rain at the end of his nose, on the wind roaring in his ears. His mom helped Norman onto the side of the road.

Norman peed into the dark ditch.

The family stood silently outside the car, Myles and his mother willing Norman to hurry up. Car exhaust blew in their faces, along with the rain. Myles counted to twenty again and again, but it was the pee to end all pees. It was never going to end. It was epic.

Hurry up, Norman!

Then … a smoky blur behind the trees! The trees swayed, a twig broke … a huge, misty head loomed above the treetops and wispy arms reached out … red eyes shone through the darkness. The monster's deep whisper filled the air....

… *I see you, Myles....*

CHAPTER 11

RED ICE!

ꝳyles tried to scream. He very, very badly wanted to call out to his mother and his little brother that they were in danger.

But he couldn't. His voice was gone. His throat was closing. He couldn't breathe. Myles squeezed his eyes tight and hugged himself as hard as he could.

... I see you, Myles....

The monster's voice floated through the trees, and long, streaming, misty arms reached out toward him. Myles bit his tongue as tears welled up beneath his eyelids. Suddenly, some-where, very, very far away, on a farm across the fields maybe, a dog barked. It made Myles feel slightly … better. Like he wasn't completely alone in the world.

You're not real! You're not real! Leave my family alone! Please, please hurry up, Norman!

It was the bravest thing he'd ever done. Myles wanted, very badly, to run into the car and hide. But he couldn't leave his mother and little brother to face the thing following him, the monster of mist and fear, alone. He stood with his arms across his chest, rain slashing his face, his eyes screwed shut, trying not to scream. He wanted to be brave. But he was frozen to the spot. Another tree snapped — the misty monster was coming.…

"Finithed!" Norman's sharp little voice called into the wind.

Myles had never moved so fast. He tore open the car door and jumped inside. His mother moved just as fast, strapping Norman into the car seat then shutting her own door. She was soaked, with rain dripping off her nose.

"Well," she said breezily, "that was an adventure!" Myles smiled weakly at her then peeked back at the woods. Misty grey arms disappeared behind the trees.

Then ... "ICE!" Norman shrieked. The trees rocked back and forth. Norman saw it too!

"DRIVE!" Myles yelped.

His mother stepped on the gas pedal, and the car lurched back onto the dark road. The wipers shrieked across the windshield.

"RED! ICE!" Norman yelled from the back seat.

"Faster, Mom!" Myles was too scared to look out the window. There was a blur beside the car. Then ...

... a deer raced onto the road, and for a moment all Myles could see was a white tail and hooves. Myles's mom slammed on the brakes, and everyone lurched forward.

Thank goodness for seatbelts, Myles thought.

"RED ICE!" Norman called out again, pointing out the front window. And Myles could see what he meant. Red eyes. The deer's eyes *were* bright red in the headlight. Just like the fox, just like the chickens.

Just like the monster out there ...

The buck turned to face them and lowered its head. Its huge antlers looked like ghostly arms reaching out to them. Myles gulped.

"Oh, it's so beautiful!" Bea said, yawning and stretching awake.

"He is handsome, isn't he?" Myles's mother said. Myles couldn't believe his ears. They thought the deer was beautiful? It loomed out of the darkness. It had red eyes, even Norman said so. It had antlers that looked like arms. It almost ran into them.

Why couldn't they see how scary the deer was?

His mother honked the horn, which sounded ridiculous and tiny against the wail of the rain and the wind. The deer looked at them for a moment then twitched its tail and moved across the road. They all watched the huge creature trot away and disappear into the dark trees.

"Goodbye, beautiful deer!" Bea called.

"'bye, bodieful deer!" Norman echoed.

"We were so lucky to see him," their mother said. She pulled Victor back onto the road and they continued on.

Lucky?

Myles frowned. They'd been driving for four days straight, and this final night, these final few hours, were worse than all the hours and days before. It was like some terrible freakish horror movie, like a journey that would never end, with the main characters stuck inside the car forever and ever, surviving one creepy near-disaster after another.

"Mom, can I turn on the radio?" Myles asked.

"Okay, something quiet. Let's see if we can just please finish this trip in peace." She eased Victor-the-Volvo down the road, slowly picking up speed. Myles fiddled with the knobs and got a weird country station that sounded weak and very far away. They drove on. Bea and Norman settled down to sleep again in the back seat.

But Myles was a ball of worry. He'd heard it.

… *I see you, Myles.…*

It wasn't just a deer. Or just a fox at Go Home Highway.

Was it?

And something with red eyes wrecked the chicken truck.

Myles needed to think about something else. With a huge effort, he forced himself to focus on the dark, rainy road ahead. Someone had to watch for more deer.…

But now there was a new worry. What if they missed the detour sign that would get them back onto the highway?

He had lost track of time with the stop for Norman and his epic pee, then the scary near-miss with the deer on the road. But it seemed like a lot longer than fifteen minutes had gone by since they started on the road. The workman back at the detour had said it would be fifteen minutes, then turn left, then …

… *what if we missed the detour? What if? We'll just drive around and around and around in the dark forever … with the monster out there following me.…*

"Mom?" It had definitely been fifteen minutes since they left the highway. They should be seeing the detour sign any minute now. Myles's mother ignored him.

"Mom?" he repeated, a little louder.

"Uh-huh?" his mother murmured.

"Mom, what if we don't find the detour sign?" There, he'd said it.

His mom didn't answer. That was just about the scariest thing she could have done. Myles turned up the radio and peeked into the back seat. Norman was fast asleep. At least he wouldn't have to pee again for a while. Bea was snoring.

Why did she get to be so peaceful? Why was SHE always so calm when Myles was a mess all the time? Didn't she realize that they were going to drive around and around on this creepy, deserted back road for the rest of their lives?

Another minute went by.

No detour sign.

Another minute.

Another minute. Another.

Myles was just about to point out the obvious (they were lost, there was no sign, they'd just keep driving around and around in the terrifying darkness forever) ...

... when his mother steered the car sharply to the left.

The fork in the road! The little red detour sign was right there! She found it!

Myles's mother smiled over at her son. "You have a very vivid imagination, Myles. You really thought we weren't going to find the detour sign? Have some faith. We're back on the highway, and we'll be home in an hour. Your dad will be so happy to see us. Go to sleep." Myles wanted to sleep, he really did. But he couldn't.

It was almost like he knew the scariest thing was still to come.

CHAPTER 12

THE MONSTER OUTSIDE

The rain had stopped, but thunder still boomed from time to time. Without the hum of the wipers, the car was oddly quiet.

Victor travelled slowly along the highway, as though Myles's mother just didn't have the heart to make the old car go too fast. The blackness outside the window was endless.

The country music radio station faded in and out. Myles could hear the funny hiss of static as the signal was lost.

Norman and Bea snored softly in the back seat.

The hiss of the radio and the gentle snoring calmed Myles. He looked over the field. His family was going to be okay. They were on the right road. Soon they'd be in Nobleville, which would be a nice alternative to living in a car for the rest of their lives. He was actually starting to WANT to get to his new home, his new town, his new school. Anything would be better than this.

Whatever is out there can't get me now, Myles thought. *All I have to do is let Mom drive a little longer, and soon this night will be behind us forever.*

He almost felt himself chuckle. Maybe it *was* kind of cool … even if Bea didn't believe it, Myles knew they saw *ghosts*. Real ones. The trip had been quite an adventure, a story to tell one day. And the monster? Well, whatever it was, it was *outside* and Myles was *inside* the car.

He let his eyes glaze over and stared out into the dark …

… TWO HUGE RED EYES glared back at him.

The monster was running along the road beside the car!

Two huge misty legs strode, wispy arms reached out, a monstrous grey head waved among the trees. Dark red eyes looked right at him.

Myles stared, too scared to scream.

The monster's eyes were red as fire, its body a dancing grey mist. Myles could faintly see the dark field behind it. A black place opened where a mouth should be....

... *I see you, Myles*....

Then the monster *leapt over the car!*

"Mom! Look out!" Myles shouted.

His mother took her eyes off the road for a second and looked at Myles. She frowned again.

"Myles, are you okay? You're white as a ... sheet." Myles was very glad his mother hadn't said "ghost."

Myles felt sick.

What if he never got rid of IT? WHAT IF THE MONSTER FOLLOWED HIM FOREVER?

His heart hammered in his chest. It was now or never. Time to tell his mother the truth. His voice was shaky and wobbly.

"Mom, there's something following me! But you can't see it! I saw a weird man, a monster, on an island from the ferry ... and I didn't tell you. But it's out there. It's following me.

It's here now!" Myles's voice shivered with fear. His mother put a hand on Myles's shoulder and tried to calm him, but it wasn't all that easy since she was driving.

"Look, I understand that you're scared about something, Myles. I'm sorry. That old man and his dog ... well, it's late. We shouldn't have driven all night, it's not fair to you and to Norman and Bea, I realize that now. I hoped you guys would just sleep, but it's been a terrible night, what with the ... *story* at the diner. And the truck wreck and the detour, then the deer. And the storm. It's all weird. Plus you're moving to a new house for the first time in your life. I'm not surprised you're upset, when you're so tired and everything is so strange. You're a sensitive boy, Myles, plus you've got a great, some might even say overactive, imagination."

Myles could feel his mother's voice soothing him. He tried to take a few deep breaths.

"It's okay to be scared of new things sometimes. But you can't let fear decide your journey, or your future. Soon we'll all be together again and this night will just be a distant memory. Hey, look!" She pointed at a green sign beside the highway as they drove past.

"Did you see that sign? It said NOBLEVILLE 65. We're almost there! We'll see Dad soon!" She sounded happy. Myles was a tiny bit relieved to see the word "Nobleville," so solidly real, on the sign. His dad and his new home weren't far. Up until now, everything had seemed so unreal.

Myles settled into his seat. His heart slowed a bit. His mom was probably right, he was just tired and weirded out. He turned his head to look out the window....

... and RED EYES popped up right beside his!

The huge misty body jumped onto the hood of the car and stared straight through the windshield! A darkly smiling mouth grinned at Myles....

See me now, Myles? it whispered.

BANGGG!

A monstrous hand slammed into the windshield, then the monster flew off into the dark.

"What on earth was that?" Myles's mother said. She pulled the car over to the side of the road.

"MOM! You saw it too! The monster!" Myles shouted. He wanted to cry, to scream, to somehow run away and hide forever. He strained his ears, but the whispery voice was gone. Then from somewhere really far away, he thought he heard a dog bark.

"Where did that huge rock come from? It broke the windshield!" his mother said. A spidery crack formed across the glass.

"A rock? It wasn't a ROCK, Mom!" Myles shouted again, almost hysterical. "It was that monster thing, the thing that's following me!" He could tell she didn't understand a word of what he was saying.

She looked at him with complete concentration and said very, very gently, "Myles, it was a rock. I saw a *rock* hit the windshield. You're seeing things. I know it's really late, and it's been a weird night, but you have to stop talking about a monster. There's no monster, Myles. Okay?"

In that moment, Myles had no choice. The monster existed, outside the car. Here, inside the car, his mother couldn't see it, couldn't hear it, like he did.

Myles was beginning to think there were lots of things she couldn't see, but he knew they were there. Like the fox. And Courage.

He nodded. He looked into the back seat where Norman and Bea were somehow still sleeping, a pile of older sister and little brother and teddy bear and Spiderman sleeping bag all knotted together.

He sighed. He was so tired. Exhausted. Maybe it didn't matter whether people could see what he saw or not. "Okay, Mom. It was a rock."

It was a monster. But if you want it to be a rock, it was a rock. I know the truth….

Myles's mother patted his shoulder then turned her attention back to the roaring car. She pressed her foot on the pedal, but nothing happened. Victor had been making weirder and weirder sounds in the last few moments.

The car coughed, then coughed again.

Then … stopped. For a moment, everything was silent.

Myles looked at his mother. His mother looked at the steering wheel.

She gritted her teeth and said, "Victor! You CANNOT DIE NOW!" She banged her hand on the steering wheel.

She turned the key.

Nothing.

She turned the key once more. Nothing. Then with a huge sigh, steam puffed up from under the hood. *That* had never happened before.

Myles and his mother watched as the crack in the windshield spread out fast across the glass in a dark, flat line. It looked like a heartbeat that had stopped forever in one of those hospital shows.

At the very moment when the patient dies.

CHAPTER 13

PARKING LOT AT THE END OF THE WORLD

Bea sat in the driver's seat, steering. Myles and his mother pushed Victor slowly along the black, silent highway. The rain had stopped but an eerie wind blew across the endless fields. Their trusty old car was really dead, and Myles and his mother had no choice but to push it off the road.

... I see you, Myles....

The monster's voice carried on the wind. The hair on Myles's neck stood up. His heart beat too fast but he shut his eyes and pushed the car. What choice did he have?

Myles was almost numb. When his mother told him he'd have to get out and help her push the car, he moved like he was in someone else's body.

Sure, Mom, he heard himself saying, *I'll go out there and help you push this enormous car into the dark night. There's a monster out there, but it's no problem.*

Myles pushed, and his running shoes squished against the wet highway.

"Mom, what time is it?" he heard a boy's voice ask, his probably.

"It's four thirty in the morning. The sun is going to come up soon," she said, panting a little as she pushed. The car rolled ever ... so ... slowly ... along.

Myles closed his eyes and pushed, grimly determined. The bushes rustled. The trees swayed. The monster whispered in the wind. Myles almost didn't care. A part of him cared, of course, very much. But a bigger part, an exhausted part, didn't. He'd given up hope of the night ever ending.

... I see you, Myles....

The constant whisper was becoming ... annoying. Almost as annoying as Norman when he sang "C! C! C!" again and again. Myles smiled darkly. If he could put up with Norman singing the same song over and over and over, for four days in the smelly car … he suddenly realized he could put up with the monster's constant whisper.

He thought his arms were going to break. He couldn't push any more … he was going to drop to his knees and die right there … the monster was going to come and swoop down on them in a misty horror.

… *I see you, Myles.*…

Myles pushed and gritted his teeth.

"M … Mom?" Myles grunted after a few minutes.

"Y … yes?" she managed to say as she pushed.

"Do … do you hear anything?" Myles asked. Sweat poured down his head and into his eyes.

"Well … yes, actually, now you ask."

"You do? What? What do you hear?"

"Well, it's strange, but I think maybe I keep hearing a dog barking, really far away. He must know that sunrise is coming soon."

A dog barking? Myles stopped pushing and was going to ask his mother what, exactly, she meant.

But before he could … a miracle happened. An old abandoned truck stop appeared at the side of the road. The truck stop was in the middle of nowhere, surrounded by empty black fields. But it had a single streetlamp, and a tiny shaft of light shone down on the broken, weedy cement below. Bea let out a little whoop of delight from inside the car. Myles and his mother pushed Victor to the island of light then leaned against the car, gasping.

Myles listened to the wind, to the silence in the fields and forests. The monster was suddenly strangely silent … but maybe there *was* a dog barking out there, somewhere really far off. He strained to hear. Yes! He could hear it!

"Where are we?" Bea asked, getting out of the car. A sign that hung from broken hinges on a signpost said DAN'S TRUCK STOP. It creaked a little in the wind.

Their mother sighed. "We're nowhere, Bea. I guess I should call for help." She got her purse from the car … then …

"Uh-oh," she whispered.

"What? What is it?" Myles asked. He didn't need any uh-ohs. Not here. Not now.

She looked at him in despair. "I forgot! The phone is almost dead. I hope I have enough battery left for one last call!" Her voice was determined, though. She marched away to a little hill, and a moment later Myles and Bea could hear her talking to someone.

Myles almost couldn't believe it. They finally had some good luck, or at least not terrible luck. His mother's cellphone had actually worked. Apparently people still existed out there somewhere. Other humans who could answer the phone and talk to you. Offer advice. Send help.

Help.

That seemed so far away, Myles couldn't even really believe it.

His mother came back and dropped her cellphone into her pocket. "Well, the tow truck will be here in two hours. We might as well get some sleep." They all climbed back into the car, and Bea and their mother both fell right to sleep, like Norman.

Not Myles, though. He sat with his eyes open, listening. It was suddenly eerily quiet outside. Too quiet. Not a bird, not a breeze, not a whisper.

But maybe ... just maybe ... a dog's bark carried on the wind.

CHAPTER 14

I'M HERE NOW, MYLES....

*S*cratch. *Scratch.*

Myles woke with a snort and sat up straight.

When did I fall asleep?

He rubbed his eyes. The clock said five thirty. It was still dark. He'd been asleep for one stupid hour. His mother was fast asleep beside him, her breath fogging the window next to her cheek.

Myles looked into the back seat.

BEA AND NORMAN WERE GONE! Myles sat bolt upright and looked outside.

WHERE WERE THEY?

"Mom! MOM!" He shook his mother gently, then …

Scratch. Scratch.

Something was scratching *just outside Myles's door.* He gulped.

Scratch. Scratch.

Scratch.

Myles sat up straighter.

"Mom? Uh … Mom?" He shook her again, a little harder this time. But his mother didn't hear him. He shook her arm. "Mom!" he said, a little louder.

"Not now, dear, I have to finish folding the laundry," his mother mumbled pleasantly.

She wasn't going to wake up. Who could blame her? She hadn't slept properly in a long time.

Scratch. Scratch.

Scratch.

Whine.

Myles clenched his fists and counted to ten. He was shaking, his arms trembled, his knees were weak … but he peeked out the car window.

And saw a nose. A DOG'S nose.

Myles gasped.

Courage! The ghostly dog seemed very real in the half-light. Courage wagged his tail then trotted across the parking lot, looking back at Myles a few times. Courage stopped at the edge of the dark woods.

Myles gulped. He really, really didn't want to go outside the car. There were lots of good reasons NOT to....

First of all, Courage was a *ghost*.

Second, *the monster* was out there.

And third, who in their right mind would follow a *ghost dog*, in the *dark of night*, in the *middle of nowhere*, with *a monster* out there?

But ... his brother and sister were out there, too.

And Courage wanted him to follow. Myles really didn't know what to do. He should probably try harder to wake up his mother, but she looked so calm and peaceful. She hadn't slept much in four days.

"If I'm ever going to be brave, I should start now," Myles said out loud. He bit his lip. He looked at the huge crack across Victor's front window. He thought about the weird night.

He was scared, yes, and exhausted. But he suddenly also felt ... a tiny bit angry. Why did the monster get to kill their faithful old car? Why did it get to scare him half to death? Why did it get to whisper spooky things again and again?

He had pushed the car through the dark night. Help was coming. He took another peek at his mother, who was snoring gently.

He knew what he had to do.

Myles carefully opened the car door.

"Okay, Courage. I'm coming," he whispered into the darkness.

Across the parking lot, Courage pricked up his ears and wagged his tail. The dog padded a little way into the forest.

It was spooky outside. And cold. Myles could see a faint pinkness in the sky to the east. The sun was coming. Not up. But soon. The wind was gentle, the sky was clear, the air was fresh and clean. Bright stars peeked out of high, thin clouds racing toward the pink dawn.

"Courage?" Myles whispered. The dog peeked out of the woods, surrounded by a gentle golden glow.

Ghosts glow, just so you know.

Myles followed, step by step, further and further away from the car, from safety. His

stomach clenched, his breathing was short and ragged. He looked back at Victor-the-Volvo parked in the little halo of light.

How he wanted to run back to the car! But he didn't. He kept going.

Courage disappeared into the dark forest. Myles hesitated. He didn't want to go in there. After this weird, long, scary night, he just couldn't.

"What am I doing? This is SO stupid!" Myles shivered at the edge of the trees. "Why am I out here?" He was just about to turn back to the car to try once again to wake his mother when very faintly, he heard the deep whisper....

... *I see them, Myles....*

Myles bolted.

He didn't stop to think. He ran into the forest. He had to save his brother and sister! He ran and stumbled past trees and logs. "Bea! Norman!" he called.

What if the monster got them? He tripped and tore the knee of his jeans, but he jumped up and kept running. Branches snagged at his shirt and hair, leaves whipped at his face and hands ... he'd never find them ... they'd vanish and it would be all his fault ...

... then there they were.

Bea and Norman stood in a clearing at the edge of the woods, holding hands. The sun was about to rise over the hill and the fields were pink and orange. Myles almost caught up with them, but not before a whispery voice said:

... *I'm here now, Myles....*

The monster was fast. It drifted across the field. The huge shape floated and stopped behind Bea, who was intently watching the sunrise. Myles watched in horror as the monster grew and grew behind her, until it was taller than the trees. Smoky arms reached out, red eyes gleamed. The monster of mist, of fog, and of fear slowly curled its wispy arms out toward Bea. The red eyes stared right at Myles....

... *I have them, Myles....*

"No! NO! GET AWAY FROM MY BROTHER AND SISTER!" Myles screamed.

He leapt into the clearing. The monster's whispery laugh chilled Myles's heart. It drew its arms closer, closer to Bea, almost stroking her hair. It whispered ...

... *She's mine now, Myles....*

But Myles didn't care. Not this time. He ran forward with a howl. He pushed his sister out of the way and screamed, "I SEE YOU, TOO!"

Furious tears burned in Myles's eyes, but he ran at the monster. He pushed, he flailed, his arms flew at … the air.

At the misty morning.

At the dew and fog and light. At the … sunshine.

"Leave them alone! Leave ME alone! LEAVE US ALONE!" In answer, Myles heard the low, deep voice laughing in the breeze. Then … a bird chirped.

A gentle ray of sun shone into the trees above the clearing and a harmless mist rose into the sky, disappearing with the gloom.

Then Bea's voice rang out. "Take it easy, little brother! It's okay! Wow, you're really upset! More upset than usual!" Bea put her arm over his shoulder to calm him down. Myles looked around.

Bea was right. Sunlight filled the clearing, the fields, the woods. Birds chirped, a squirrel ran right past them to start a busy day. Norman slipped his hand into Myles's.

"Ith okay, Myles. Look! The thun!" Norman pointed at the light. Myles nodded.

Sunlight broke over the hills. At the very edge of the woods, the faint outline of a beautiful dog formed in the mist one last time. Myles strained to hear a faraway bark on the wind.

Then the mist vanished as the early morning sunlight burned away the last wisps of night.

CHAPTER 15

PRINTS AND PAWS

Norman held Myles's hand all the way back to the parking lot. There was a perfectly nice path that Myles hadn't seen in the dark.

The world hadn't changed.

Except it had. The sun was up. The sky was bright and clear.

And the terrible night was over. Myles was exhausted. He felt empty. He had no idea being brave would be so tiring. Birds were singing in the forest. There wasn't a cloud in the pink early morning sky.

"Are you okay, Myles?" Bea asked as they walked.

"I ... I don't know." Here in the early morning light, in the quiet beautiful forest, he wasn't sure. Maybe. Maybe he was okay. He suddenly wanted to tell her everything, about the monster, about Courage, about his fears about their new house, and about being so mad at their dad for making them move. But he couldn't, not right now. One day maybe, but right now he was too tired.

"Why were you out of the car?" Myles asked after a few more steps.

"Norman woke me up."

"I hadz to pee again," Norman nodded.

"You and Mom looked so peaceful, I didn't want to wake you. I took Norman outside, then we went to see the sunrise. You know, the back seat really stinks. How did you manage to sit back there for so long?" Bea's voice was so normal, so ... Bea.

She was amazing. Wasn't she afraid of *anything*? Who else would get out of a car in the dark to wander through a pitch black forest to help Norman? And look at the sunrise?

Then Myles realized with a start that there *was* someone else. Him. He would. He *did*.

He didn't get to think about that for too long, though. Suddenly, a loud horn beeped as a tow truck pulled into the parking lot. A tall man in overalls got out and knocked on the car window.

Their mother burst out of her side of the car, sleepy and mussed up.

"Thank you for coming," she said, straightening her hair. "You've caught me sleeping. My kids and I had a long, long night last night." Myles and his brother and sister walked over to join them.

"Sorry I took so long to get here, I had to tow a wrecked chicken truck to the junkyard this morning. The darnedest thing —"

"Yes! Thank you, we know about the chicken truck," Myles's mother said, stopping him. Clearly, she didn't want to hear any more about Mr. Chicken Truck Man.

The tow truck driver walked around the car, then he stopped and whistled. He pointed at the crack in the windshield.

"Whoa, what a huge crack!"

"Yes, a big rock hit us hard, right before the car died," their mother answered.

Monster, Mom. Not a rock.

The man nodded then pointed at the mud and gravel beside the car.

"And look! Huge footprints. See? They're all around the car." The man walked around Victor, pointing at the ground. Then he pointed toward the woods.

"The footprints go off in that direction." Everyone walked to the edge of the trees, Bea holding Norman's hand.

Very slowly, Myles joined them.

The man pointed at the mud between the woods and the parking lot. Then Myles saw them: gigantic, swirling footprints in the mud.

"I — I've seen those prints before," the man said slowly.

"What is it?" Myles's mother asked, but the man didn't answer.

"There's another track beside it," he went on. "A pawprint, see the four pads? It looks like a big dog."

"Well, what happened?" Myles's mother asked, bewildered.

The tow truck driver shook his head a little. "I'm not really sure, ma'am. It looks like something big, something REALLY big, was sniffing beside your car. Then over here, you can see the dog pawprints are all mixed up with the huge footprints. If I had to guess, I'd say a dog chased whatever was sniffing at your car off into the woods."

The man narrowed his eyes a little, looking right at Myles. "You're SURE you didn't see anything or hear anything last night? There was something sniffing at your car door and fighting with a big dog, right here."

"No, no honestly. We didn't hear anything, did we? Myles? Bea? We all just fell right to sleep. It's a mystery," their mother said.

It's not a mystery! A deep chill started at Myles's toes and moved up to his chest, then to the top of his head.

The man put his oily mechanic hands on his hips. Then he cleared his throat, like he didn't want to say what was coming next.

"There's something else you should know. Those huge strange footprints ... I saw them all around the wrecked chicken truck last night. They were *just like these*."

"Well, what are they?" Myles's mother asked again, but the man just shrugged.

"I have no idea, ma'am."

I do. I know exactly what put those footprints there! Myles wanted to scream.

Bea's reasonable voice broke the silence.

"Well, there's something *we* should tell *you*. We saw Pete Fournette last night," she said matter-of-factly. "And although I don't happen to think any of that 'ghost walks the highway' story is real, my brother thinks he saw Pete's dog. What was his name again, Myles?"

"Courage," Myles said, quietly. The man stood up and raised his eyebrows. He whistled and nodded softly.

"We-lll ... isn't THAT interesting! I haven't heard anyone mention Pete Fournette in a LONG time. Years. And I've NEVER heard anyone talk about seeing his dog. Courage, did you say? That's a first."

Everyone looked at Myles. He got the uncomfortable feeling, once again, that no one really believed him about Courage. Pawprints were one thing, seeing a ghost dog was another. Suddenly he didn't care. So what if no one else could see Courage?

Myles knew he was out there. Somewhere. He might be the only person who could see the monster, but he was the only person who could see the ghost dog, too. Maybe seeing things wasn't all bad.

The tow truck driver broke the silence. "Well, something big was chased off into the woods by a dog, no doubt about it. And whatever it was, the same thing ran the chicken truck off the road a few hours earlier." The man put his hands on his hips and looked at the footprints at their feet.

Myles's mother and Bea stared at him like they didn't understand. Or at this point in the long, long night, maybe they just didn't want to.

But Myles understood. Perfectly.

The monster chased us all night.

But Courage chased it away, every time it came near.

It couldn't wreck us, so the monster wrecked the chicken truck instead.

They all fell silent, too tired to talk as the driver hooked Victor up to the back of his tow truck. A few times Myles peeked over at the woods, but nothing moved except birds and squirrels.

It seemed impossible that the night was really over, but somehow it was. A few minutes later, everyone climbed into the truck and they drove onto the highway, towing Victor behind them like a brave fallen soldier on wheels.

As they drove away, Myles looked out the back window. He couldn't help it. He peeked … and there it was….

A dark mist curled out of the woods and formed silently around two red, staring eyes. A deep voice whispered into the quiet morning …

…. *I'll find you, Myles….*

Myles raised his chin. *Maybe,* he thought. *But next time I'll know you. Next time, I'll be ready.*

And this time there was no mistake. Outside, a dog's bark rose on the breeze.

THIS PART IS ALSO (MOSTLY) TRUE

Welcome to the end of the story, and if you've made it this far, congratulations. I told you at the beginning that it was scary and more than a little strange, and yet here you are. I'm sure you'll never go on a long drive again without wondering what might be following you in the dark fields, out of sight.

Out of everyone's sight but yours, of course.

You've no doubt got many questions at this point. You're probably wondering what happened next? And you might just be thinking … is this story *true*?

But if you remember, on the very first pages of this story you read these words: *Truth is an odd thing; one person's truth can be another person's lie. That's the most important thing to remember about this story: sometimes things that seem like lies are actually true. And sometimes you never can tell.*

I could leave the story right there, and you'd just have to accept it. But that would be unfair of me, and I pride myself on being fair.

So, without further ado, here are the answers you seek....

Myles and his family *did* make it to their new home. An hour after climbing into the tow truck, they stood in front of a beautiful house. Their house.

There were no broken doors squeaking on hinges, no hanging windows or huge black crows CAW! CAWing from dark trees. Instead, the house was tall and newly painted with big windows, and a large front balcony with a hammock that would soon be eternally swinging. If you were looking for Bea, for instance, she was probably in the hammock reading.

And inside the house? Inside the house that morning, their dad was waiting for them all with pancakes ... as he promised. He swept

Norman into his arms and hugged Bea. He ruffled Myles's hair.

"You've grown, Myles!" he said.

Myles nodded. Yeah. He had. Myles *had* grown. A lot. On the outside maybe, and in ways you couldn't see, too.

And the "surprise" his dad had for him? You can probably guess, but it's a nice surprise all the same: a dog. Myles was finally going to have his own dog. I'm not even going to tell you what he named it, because surely you can guess.

As they built their lives in their new town, Myles and his family prospered.

They DID get a new car but kept Victor-the-Volvo in the driveway for years, because they couldn't bear to say goodbye.

Myles DID start to enjoy things like his own music and his own room, although he found he didn't mind so much if Norman felt like singing his song about C! C! C! now and then, or if he wanted to sleep in Myles's room on dark, rainy nights once in a while.

He really DID start to like his new home, his new school, and his new town. All those worries, gone, gone, gone.

But more than all that, you're probably curious about Pete Fournette and his dog Courage. Were they really ghosts?

There's plenty of evidence for the ghost story, at the diner and in the library archives, isn't there? Mrs. Cody the librarian and plenty of other adults seemed to think it was true, even if Bea didn't. And then there's the fact that Courage was glowing each time Myles saw him (and ghosts DO glow, you know, at least some of them do).

The truth is, as far as I know, after Myles and his family saw him, old Pete never wandered the rainy April highway ever again.

Why?

Well, I think it's because he finally heard the answer he'd longed for.

Pete had asked people the same question for over one hundred years: *Have you seen my dog?*

No one had.

Until someone did.

Myles. After all those years of saying "no," someone finally answered "yes" to Pete's question, and so his restless wandering spirit grew still.

Well, not completely still. There are those who will tell you that on a perfect spring night when the trees blow gently and anything is possible, you may see an old man and a beautiful golden dog walking along the highway, together at last. If you're very quiet, you may hear a faraway dog's bark. And if you are especially lucky, you may even hear an old man's pleasant whisper: *Come, Courage, it's time for home ...*

And the monster outside? Was it really there? Did it really follow Myles all that long, long night? Did it ever find him again?

Despite the scary whispers, Victor's broken window, the footprints in the mud ... was it a monster that Myles saw? Or anxiety about moving, exhaustion, and a bad storm mixed together with a fox in the bushes of an old farmhouse, the antlers of a deer, a rock?

In the end, only Myles really knows.

I CAN tell you that if Myles was bothered by a big worry, like a final chemistry exam or the time he had pneumonia one winter, misty fingers *would* snake out of the woods behind his house. Red eyes *did* blaze in the dark, and a deep voice *would* whisper... *I'm here now, Myles ...*

... but Myles would count to ten. Take a deep breath. Decide not to be afraid. Sometimes the monster left right away, sometimes it didn't, but it didn't really matter.

Because Courage was out there, too.

So now you know the story of Myles and the monster outside. Despite his possibly overactive imagination and his many fears, he grew up in a perfectly ordinary way.

There were only two things that were a little odd about Myles.

One: his father gave him his first dog, and he was never without one for the rest of his life. He sometimes had two, or even three dogs at a time. They all had the same name, which got a bit confusing if, say, you were trying to get just one of them to come to you. (I'm sure you can guess what they were all named.)

Two: If you ever whispered around Myles, for a moment he'd get a wild look on his face then say quietly, "I see you, too … and I'm NOT afraid!"

They're troubling. They're bizarre.
And they JUST might be true …

Weird Stories Gone Wrong

BY PHILIPPA DOWDING

BOOK 1
The ghastly truth about
a giant hand …

BOOK 2
A rainy night,
a haunted highway,
a mysterious monster …

BOOK 3
Are you brave enough to
enter the curious maze?
Not everyone comes out …

Three tremendously terrifying tales you'll want to share with
your enemies (should you want to scare them silly) …

Available at your favourite bookseller